対 訳

21世紀に生きる君たちへ
司馬遼太郎

ドナルド・キーン監訳／ロバート・ミンツァー訳

朝日出版社

目 次 Contents

人間の荘厳さ …2
　The Magnificence of Humanity …3

21世紀に生きる君たちへ …4
　To You Who Will Live in the 21st Century …5

洪庵のたいまつ …22
　The Torch of Koan …23

人間の荘厳さ

　人間は、鎖の一環ですね。はるかな過去から未来にのびてゆく鎖の。——人間のすばらしさは、自分のことを、たかが一環かとは悲観的におもわないことです。ふしぎなものですね。たとえば、小さい人たちは、いきいきと伸びてゆこうとしています。少年少女が、いまの一瞬を経験するとき、過去や現在のたれとも無関係な、真新の、自分だけの心の充実だとおもっているのです。荘厳なものですね。

　「21世紀に生きる君たちへ」は、そういう荘厳さを感じつつ、書いたのです。つぎの鎖へ、ひとりずつへの手紙として。こればかりは時世時節を超越して不変のものだということを書きました。日本だけでなく、アフリカのムラや、ニューヨークの街にいるこどもにも通じるか、おそらく通じる、と何度も自分に念を押しつつ書きました。

The Magnificence of Humanity

Each human being is a link in a chain—a chain that extends from the distant past into the future. Human greatness lies in not regarding one's existence pessimistically as merely a link in the chain. It's really strange. Consider, for example, how young people strive so vigorously to grow up. Each instant that boys and girls experience, they feel an inner fulfillment that is theirs alone, brand new and unconnected to anyone else either past or present. This is magnificent indeed.

It was in awe of that magnificence that I wrote "To You Who Will Live in the 21st Century." I wrote it as a letter to each person who will form a next link in the chain. I wrote that this alone is unchangeable, transcending time and season. As I wrote it, I told myself time and again that its message would—or probably would—apply to children not only in Japan but also in African villages or the streets of New York.

21世紀に生きる君たちへ

　私は、歴史小説を書いてきた。

　もともと歴史が好きなのである。両親を愛するようにして、歴史を愛している。

　歴史とはなんでしょう、と聞かれるとき、
「それは、大きな世界です。かつて存在した何億という人生がそこにつめこまれている世界なのです。」
と、答えることにしている。

　私には、幸い、この世にたくさんのすばらしい友人がいる。

　歴史の中にもいる。そこには、この世では求めがたいほどにすばらしい人たちがいて、私の日常を、はげましたり、なぐさめたりしてくれているのである。

　だから、私は少なくとも二千年以上の時間の中を、生きているようなものだと思っている。この楽しさは——もし君たちさえそう望むなら——おすそ分けしてあげたいほどである。

　ただ、さびしく思うことがある。

To You Who Will Live in the 21st Century

I have been a writer of historical fiction. I have always liked history. I love history the way I love my parents. Whenever I am asked what history is, I always reply that it's a big world, a world crammed with the lives of the billions of people who lived before us.

I am lucky in having many wonderful friends in this world.

I have some in history too. There are wonderful people there, people it would be hard to find in this world, and they encourage me and comfort me in my daily life. As a result, I feel I am living within a period of time over two thousand years long, at the very least. I would like to share this pleasure with you, if that is what you'd like.

One thing makes me sad, though. There is something big

私が持っていなくて、君たちだけが持っている大きなものがある。未来というものである。
　私の人生は、すでに持ち時間が少ない。例えば、21世紀というものを見ることができないにちがいない。
　君たちは、ちがう。
　21世紀をたっぷり見ることができるばかりか、そのかがやかしいにない手でもある。

　もし「未来」という町角で、私が君たちを呼びとめることができたら、どんなにいいだろう。
「田中君、ちょっとうかがいますが、あなたが今歩いている21世紀とは、どんな世の中でしょう。」
　そのように質問して、君たちに教えてもらいたいのだが、ただ残念にも、その「未来」という町角には、私はもういない。
　だから、君たちと話ができるのは、今のうちだということである。

　もっとも、私には21世紀のことなど、とても予測できない。
　ただ、私に言えることがある。それは、歴史から学んだ人間の

which I don't have but you do: a future. I don't have much longer to live. For example, I am sure I won't be able to see the 21st century.

But you will. You will not only live to see your fill of the 21st century, but you will be its splendid leaders.

How nice it would be if I could stop you on a street corner called "the future" and say, "Excuse me, young Mr. Tanaka. What kind of world is the 21st century where you are living now?" I would like to ask you a question like that and learn the answer from you, but unfortunately I will no longer be on that street corner called the future. That's why it's only now, while I'm still here, that I can talk with you.

Of course, I am altogether unable to predict what the 21st century will be like. But there is something I can speak on.

生き方の基本的なことどもである。

　昔も今も、また未来においても変わらないことがある。そこに空気と水、それに土などという自然があって、人間や他の動植物、さらには微生物(びせいぶつ)にいたるまでが、それに依存(いそん)しつつ生きているということである。
　自然こそ不変の価値なのである。なぜならば、人間は空気を吸うことなく生きることができないし、水分をとることがなければ、かわいて死んでしまう。
　さて、自然という「不変のもの」を基準に置いて、人間のことを考えてみたい。
　人間は、──くり返すようだが──自然によって生かされてきた。古代でも中世でも自然こそ神々であるとした。このことは、少しも誤っていないのである。歴史の中の人々は、自然をおそれ、その力をあがめ、自分たちの上にあるものとして身をつつしんできた。
　この態度は、近代や現代に入って少しゆらいだ。
──人間こそ、いちばんえらい存在だ。

This is the basic way for a human being to live, which I have learned from history.

In the ancient past and today, as well as in the future, there are some things that do not change. Among them is the existence of Nature—air, water, soil and such—and the fact that man, other animals, plants and even microorganisms rely on it to live. Nature has unchanging value. This is because man cannot live without breathing air, and unless he consumes water he becomes parched and dies. Here, I would like to think about man, using Nature, this "unchanging thing," as a yardstick.

Humans—though I may seem to repeat myself—are kept alive by Nature. In ancient times and in the Middle Ages, Nature was equated with gods. This is not wrong even slightly. People in history always feared Nature, respected its power, and behaved cautiously in the belief that Nature was something that is above them. This attitude wavered a little in modern and contemporary times. The conceited notion that it is man who is

という、思いあがった考えが頭をもたげた。20世紀という現代は、ある意味では、自然へのおそれがうすくなった時代といっていい。

　同時に、人間は決しておろかではない。思いあがるということとはおよそ逆のことも、あわせ考えた。つまり、私ども人間とは自然の一部にすぎない、というすなおな考えである。
　このことは、古代の賢者(けんじゃ)も考えたし、また19世紀の医学もそのように考えた。ある意味では平凡(へいぼん)な事実にすぎないこのことを、20世紀の科学は、科学の事実として、人々の前にくりひろげてみせた。
　20世紀末の人間たちは、このことを知ることによって、古代や中世に神をおそれたように、再び自然をおそれるようになった。
　おそらく、自然に対しいばりかえっていた時代は、21世紀に近づくにつれて、終わっていくにちがいない。

「人間は、自分で生きているのではなく、大きな存在によって生かされている。」

the greatest thing in existence reared its head. This contemporary era called the 20th century in a sense might be called the period in which the fear of Nature weakened.

At the same time, man is by no means a fool. He also thought almost the exact opposite of being conceited: namely, the idea that we human beings are merely one part of Nature.

This was what the wise men of ancient days also thought, and how 19th-century medical science thought of it too. This idea, which in a sense is nothing more than a common fact, was unfolded before people as scientific fact by 20th-century science.

People of the late 20th century, with knowledge of this fact, again came to fear Nature in the way people feared gods in ancient times and the Middle Ages. Probably, the period in which man lorded it over Nature will surely come to an end as time draws increasingly close to the 21st century.

と、中世の人々は、ヨーロッパにおいても東洋においても、そのようにへりくだって考えていた。

この考えは、近代に入ってゆらいだとはいえ、右に述べたように、近ごろ再び、人間たちはこのよき思想を取りもどしつつあるように思われる。

この自然へのすなおな態度こそ、21世紀への希望であり、君たちへの期待でもある。そういうすなおさを君たちが持ち、その気分をひろめてほしいのである。

そうなれば、21世紀の人間は、よりいっそう自然を尊敬することになるだろう。そして、自然の一部である人間どうしについても、前世紀にもまして尊敬し合うようになるのにちがいない。そのようになることが、君たちへの私の期待でもある。

さて、君たち自身のことである。

君たちは、いつの時代でもそうであったように、自己を確立せねばならない。

——自分に厳しく、相手にはやさしく。

という自己を。

"Human beings do not live on their own, but are kept alive by a great presence."

This is how people in the Middle Ages, both in Europe and in the Orient, humbly thought. Although this thinking wavered after the arrival of modern times, in recent times human beings appear to be returning again to this good idea. This humble attitude toward Nature represents hope for the 21st century and the aspiration I have for you. I want you to have that kind of humility and to spread that feeling around. If you do, then the human beings of the 21st century will have even more respect for Nature. Then between humans, who are a part of Nature, there will surely be greater respect than in the previous century. For this to happen is also my aspiration for you.

Now, I will turn to you, yourselves. You, as has been so in all ages, must establish a self—a self that must be strict toward yourself, and kind toward others. And a self that is honest and wise. This will be especially important in the 21st century. In

そして、すなおでかしこい自己を。

　21世紀においては、特にそのことが重要である。

　21世紀にあっては、科学と技術がもっと発達するだろう。科学・技術が、こう水のように人間をのみこんでしまってはならない。川の水を正しく流すように、君たちのしっかりした自己が、科学と技術を支配し、よい方向に持っていってほしいのである。

　右において、私は「自己」ということをしきりに言った。自己といっても、自己中心におちいってはならない。

　人間は、助け合って生きているのである。

　私は、人という文字を見るとき、しばしば感動する。ななめの画(かく)がたがいに支え合って、構成されているのである。

　そのことでも分かるように、人間は、社会をつくって生きている。社会とは、支え合う仕組みということである。

　原始時代の社会は小さかった。家族を中心とした社会だった。それがしだいに大きな社会になり、今は、国家と世界という社会をつくり、たがいに助け合いながら生きているのである。

　自然物としての人間は、決して孤立(こりつ)して生きられるようにはつくられていない。

the 21st century, science and technology will develop further. Science and technology cannot be allowed to swallow up human beings like a flood. I want that your firm selves will take control over science and technology and take it in the right direction, like setting the course of a river properly.

Above, I frequently spoke about the "self." But though I have spoken of a self, it is wrong to slip into self-centeredness. Humans live by helping one another. When I look at the character for person, *hito*, I am frequently moved. It is composed of two slanting lines supporting each other. As we can understand from this too, human beings live by forming a society. A society refers to an arrangement of mutual support. The society of primitive times was small. It was a society centered on the family. It gradually became a big society, and now we form societies called nations and the world, and we live by helping one another.

Man, as a natural being, was definitely not made to be able to live in isolation.

このため、助け合う、ということが、人間にとって、大きな道徳になっている。
　助け合うという気持ちや行動のもとのもとは、いたわりという感情である。
　他人の痛みを感じることと言ってもいい。
　やさしさと言いかえてもいい。
「いたわり」
「他人の痛みを感じること」
「やさしさ」
　みな似たような言葉である。
　この三つの言葉は、もともと一つの根から出ているのである。
　根といっても、本能ではない。だから、私たちは訓練をしてそれを身につけねばならないのである。
　その訓練とは、簡単なことである。例えば、友達がころぶ。ああ痛かったろうな、と感じる気持ちを、そのつど自分の中でつくりあげていきさえすればよい。
　この根っこの感情が、自己の中でしっかり根づいていけば、他民族へのいたわりという気持ちもわき出てくる。

Because of this, helping one another is a great moral virtue for human beings. The original origin of feelings and actions of helping one another is the sentiment called compassion. We might also speak of it as feeling the pain of others. Another way to call it might be kindness. "Compassion." "Feeling the pain of others." "Kindness." They are all similar types of expression. All three expressions originally derive from one root.

Though I say root, it isn't an instinct. That's why we have to train to acquire it.

The training is simple. For example, a friend stumbles. All you have to do is to develop within you, each time, a feeling that "Oh, that must have hurt." When that root of sentiment takes firm root within your self, a feeling of compassion toward other races will spring forth. So long as you make that kind of self, the 21st century will surely become an age in which mankind will be able to live in harmony.

君たちさえ、そういう自己をつくっていけば、21世紀は人類が仲よしで暮らせる時代になるのにちがいない。

　鎌倉(かまくら)時代の武士たちは、
「たのもしさ」
ということを、たいせつにしてきた。人間は、いつの時代でもたのもしい人格を持たねばならない。人間というのは、男女とも、たのもしくない人格にみりょくを感じないのである。

　もう一度くり返そう。さきに私は自己を確立せよ、と言った。自分に厳しく、相手にはやさしく、とも言った。いたわりという言葉も使った。それらを訓練せよ、とも言った。それらを訓練することで、自己が確立されていくのである。そして、〝たのもしい君たち〟になっていくのである。

　以上のことは、いつの時代になっても、人間が生きていくうえで、欠かすことができない心がまえというものである。
　君たち。君たちはつねに晴れあがった空のように、たかだかとした心を持たねばならない。

The samurai warriors of the Kamakura period put much importance on the idea of "trustworthiness."

People, in all eras, must have a trustworthy character. Human beings, both men and women, do not find an untrustworthy character attractive.

Let's repeat this once again. Before, I told you to establish a self. I also told you to be strict toward yourself and kind toward others. I also used the word "compassion." And I told you to train in those things. By training in them, your self will become established. Then, you will all become "trustworthy people."

What I have written above is a frame of mind that, in whatever era may come, is indispensable for human beings to live. All of you. You must have a lofty heart, like a sky that is always clear.

同時に、ずっしりとたくましい足どりで、大地をふみしめつつ歩かねばならない。
　私は、君たちの心の中の最も美しいものを見続けながら、以上のことを書いた。
　書き終わって、君たちの未来が、真夏の太陽のようにかがやいているように感じた。

At the same time, you must tread the Earth with a firm and sturdy gait.

I wrote the above looking continuously at the most beautiful thing in your hearts. After writing it, I have come to feel that your future is shining like the midsummer sun.

洪庵のたいまつ

世のためにつくした人の一生ほど、美しいものはない。

ここでは、特に美しい生涯を送った人について語りたい。

緒方洪庵のことである。

この人は、江戸末期に生まれた。

医者であった。

かれは、名を求めず、利を求めなかった。

あふれるほどの実力がありながら、しかも他人のために生き続けた。そういう生涯は、はるかな山河のように、実に美しく思えるのである。

といって、洪庵は変人ではなかった。どの村やどの町内にもいそうな、ごくふつうのおだやかな人がらの人だった。

病人には親切で、その心はいつも愛に満ちていた。

かれの医学は、当時ふつうの医学だった漢方ではなく、世間でもめずらしいとされていたオランダ医学（蘭方）だった。そのころ、洪庵のような医者は、蘭方医とよばれていた。

変人でこそなかったが、蘭方などをやっているということで、

The Torch of Koan

Nothing is more beautiful than a life devoted to the world. Here, I want to write about a person who lived a particularly beautiful life. He is Koan Ogata.

He was born in the late Edo period. He was a doctor. He did not seek fame, nor did he seek personal gain. He had overflowing talent and continued to live for others. That kind of life seems truly beautiful, like distant mountains and rivers.

And yet, Koan was not an eccentric person. He was an extremely ordinary person of gentle character as you might find in any village or any town. He was kind to the sick, and his heart was always filled with love. The medicine he practiced was not the Chinese medicine common in those times, but Dutch medicine, which was considered quite rare by everyone. Doctors like Koan were called "doctors of Dutch medicine."

Though he wasn't an eccentric, Koan may have been thought of as "an odd person" because of the fact that he practiced the

近所の人たちから、

「変わったお人やな。」

と思われていたかもしれない。ついでながら、洪庵は大坂（今の大阪市）に住んでいた。なにしろ洪庵は、日常、人々にとって見慣れない横文字（オランダ語）の本を読んでいるのである。いっぱんの人から見れば、常人のようには思われなかったかもしれない。

洪庵は、備中（今の岡山県）の人である。現在の岡山市の西北方に足守という町があるが、江戸時代、ここに足守藩という小さな藩があって、緒方家は代々そこの藩士だった。

父が、藩の仕事で大坂に住んだために、洪庵もこの都市で過ごした。少年のころ、一人前のさむらいになるために、漢学の塾やけん術の道場に通ったのだが、生まれつき体が弱く、病気がちで、塾や道場をしばしば休んだ。少年の洪庵にとって、病弱である自分が歯がゆかった。この体、なんとかならないものだろうかと思った。

likes of Dutch medicine. Incidentally, Koan was living in Osaka (the current city of Osaka). Anyway, Koan spent his days reading books in horizontal script (Dutch), which was unfamiliar to people. In the eyes of the average person, he may not have been thought of as an ordinary person.

Koan came from Bitchu (now Okayama Prefecture). In the northwest of today's Okayama City is a town called Ashimori, and in the Edo period there was a small feudal domain here called Ashimori-han; the Ogata family served the domain generation after generation. Because his father lived in Osaka for his work for the domain, Koan lived in that city too. When he was a boy, in order to become a worthy samurai, he attended a private school for Chinese studies and trained in Kendo fencing at a dojo. But by birth he was physically weak and prone to illness, and he often stayed home from school or the dojo. For the young Koan, being sickly was irritating. He wondered if there wasn't something that could be done about

人間は、人なみでない部分をもつということは、すばらしいことなのである。そのことが、ものを考えるばねになる。

　少年時代の洪庵も、そうだった。かれは、人間について考えた。人間が健康であったり、健康でなかったり、また病気をしたりするということは、いったい何に原因するのか。さらには、人体というのはどういう仕組みになっているのだろう、というようなことを考えこんだ。

　この少年は、ものごとを理づめで考えるたちだった。

　今の言葉でいえば、科学的に考えることが好きだったといっていい。

　少年は、蘭学特に蘭方医学を学びたいと思った。

　幸い、この当時、中天游（一七八三～一八三五年）という学者が、大坂で蘭方医学の塾を開いていて、あわせて初歩的な物理学や化学についても教えていた。

　少年はここに入門した。主として医学を学んだのである。

his body.

When a person has part of him which is out of the ordinary, this is a wonderful thing. This serves as a springboard for thinking. This was how it was with Koan during his boyhood. He thought about human beings. He wondered what on earth could be the cause for people being healthy sometimes and unhealthy or sick at others.

Furthermore, he thought deeply about such things as how the human body works.

By nature, this young boy thought about things in logical terms. In today's words, we could say he liked to think "scientifically." The boy decided he wanted to learn Dutch studies, especially Dutch medicine. Fortunately, at the time a scholar named Ten'yu Naka (1783-1835) was operating a private school of Dutch medicine in Osaka, and it also taught rudimentary physics and chemistry. The young boy enrolled here. Chiefly, he studied medicine.

中天游からすべてを学び取った後、さらに師を求めて江戸へ行った。二十二才のときであった。

　江戸では、働きながら学んだ。あんまをしてわずかな金をもらったり、他家のげんかん番をしたりした。

　そのころ、江戸第一の蘭方医学の大家は、坪井信道（一七九五〜一八四八年）という人だった。

　ついでながら、江戸時代の習慣として、えらい学者は、ふつう、その自たくを塾にして、自分の学問を年わかい人々に伝えるのである。それが、社会に対する恩返しとされていた。

　洪庵は、坪井信道の塾で四年間学び、ついにオランダ語のむずかしい本まで読むことができるようになった。

　そのあと、長崎へ行った。

　長崎。

　この町についてあらかじめ知っておかねばならないことは、江戸時代が鎖国（外国と付き合わないこと）だったことである。

　幕府は、長崎港一か所を外国に対して開いていた。その外国も限られていて、アジアの国々では中国（当時は清国）だけであ

After he learned everything from Ten'yu Naka, he went to Edo to search for a new mentor. He was 22 years old. In Edo, he studied while working. At times he earned modest sums as a masseur, at others worked as a doorkeeper at people's homes.

At the time, the foremost authority on Dutch medicine in Edo was a man named Shindo Tsuboi (1795-1848).

Incidentally, it was customary in the Edo period for a great scholar normally to use his home as a private school, and to pass on his knowledge to young people. This was seen as their way of repaying their moral debt to society. Koan studied at Shindo Tsuboi's private school for four years, and in the end he became able to read even difficult books in Dutch.

After that, he went to Nagasaki. Nagasaki: What we have to know about this city first is that in the Edo period Japan was in national seclusion (had no contacts with other countries). The Bakufu government opened only one place to foreign countries: the port of Nagasaki. The foreign countries were also limited:

り、ヨーロッパの国々ではオランダだけだった。そういうわけで、長崎にはオランダ人がごく少数ながら住んでいたのである。

　もう少し鎖国（さこく）について話したい。

　鎖国というのは、例えば、日本人全部が真っ暗な箱の中にいるようなものだったと考えればいい。

　長崎（ながさき）は、箱の中の日本としては、はりでついたように小さなあなだったといえる。その小あなからかすかに世界の光が差しこんできていたのである。当時の学問好きの人々にとって、その光こそ中国であり、ヨーロッパであった。

　人々にとって、志さえあれば、暗い箱の中でも世界を知ることができる。例えば、オランダ語を学び、オランダの本を読むことによって、ヨーロッパの科学のいくぶんかでも自分のものにすることができたのである。洪庵（こうあん）もそういう青年の一人だった。洪庵は長崎の町で二年学んだ。

　二十九才のとき、洪庵は大坂にもどった。ここでしんりょうをする一方、塾（じゅく）を開いた。ほぼ同時に結こんもした。妻は、八重（やえ）と

among Asian countries, only China (Qing China at the time), and among European countries, only Holland. For this reason, Dutch people were living in Nagasaki, albeit few in number.

I want to talk about national seclusion a little more. National seclusion can be compared, for example, to a situation in which all Japanese people are inside a totally dark box. For Japan inside the box, Nagasaki was like a small hole pricked open by a needle. Through that small hole, the light of the world shined in faintly. For people of those days fond of learning, that light was China and Europe. Even inside the dark box, it was possible for people, so long as one had ambition, to know about the world. For example, by studying Dutch and reading books from Holland, it was possible to acquire knowledge, at least in part, of European science. Koan was one such young man. Kôan studied in the city of Nagasaki for two years.

When he was 29, Koan returned to Osaka. Here, he practiced medicine and also opened a private school. At almost the same

いう、やさしくて物静かな女性だった。考え深くもあった。八重は終生、かれを助け、塾の書生たちからも母親のようにしたわれた。

　洪庵は、自分の塾の名を適塾(てきじゅく)と名付けた。
　日本の近代が大きなげき場とすれば、明治(めいじ)はそのはなやかなまく開けだった。その前の江戸(えど)末期は、はいゆうたちのけいこの期間だったといえる。適塾は、日本の近代のためのけいこ場の一つになったのである。

　すばらしい学校だった。
　入学試験などはない。
　どのわか者も、勉強したくて、遠い地方から、はるばるやってくるのである。
　江戸(えど)時代は身分差別の社会だった。しかしこの学校では、いっさい平等であった。さむらいの子もいれば町医者の子もおり、また農民の子もいた。ここでは、「学問をする」というただ一つの目的と心で結ばれていた。
　適塾(てきじゅく)においては、最初の数年は、オランダ語を学ぶことについ

time, he also got married. His wife was a kind and quiet woman named Yae. She was also a deep-thinking person. Yae helped him all her life, and she was loved by the students like a mother. Koan named his school "Tekijuku."

If Japan's modern era were likened to a big theater, Meiji was the gala rising of the curtain. The late Edo period before it can be said to have been the actors' rehearsal period. Tekijuku became one of the rehearsal studios for Japan's modern era.

It was a wonderful school. There were no entrance tests. Young people of every kind, if they wanted to study, would make their way here over great distances, from far regions.

The Edo period was a time of class discrimination. But at this school, all people were equal. There were children of samurai, children of city doctors, and children of peasant farmers. Here, they were all bound by a single purpose and mind: to learn.

At Tekijuku, the first few years were spent studying Dutch.

やされる。

　先生は、洪庵しかいない。

　その洪庵先生も、病人たちをしんりょうしながら教える。体が二つあっても足りないほどいそがしかったが、それでも塾の教育はうまくいった。塾生のうちで、よくできる者ができない者を教えたからである。

　八つの級に分かれていて、適塾に入って早々の者は八級とよばれる。一級の人は、最も古いし、オランダ語もよくできる。各級に、学級委員のように「会頭」という者がいる。塾生全部の代表として、塾頭という者がいた。ある時期の塾頭として、後に明治陸軍をつくることになる大村益次郎がいたし、また別の時期の塾頭として、後に慶應義塾大学のそう立者になる福沢諭吉もいた。

　適塾の建物は、今でも残っている。場所は、大阪市中央区北浜三丁目である。

　当時、そのあたりは商家がのきをならべていて、適塾の建物はその間にはさまれていた。造りも商家風で、今日の学校という感じのものではない。門もなければ運動場もなく、あるのは二階建

Koan was the only teacher. And even Koan taught in between treating sick people. He was so busy that even two bodies would not have been enough, but even so, education at the school went smoothly. This is because the bright students helped those less clever. They were divided into eight levels, and those new to Tekijuku were called Level 8. The people in Level 1 were the oldest, and they knew Dutch well. In each level, there was a "class president," who was like a class representative. As representative of all students, there was also a person called the "school president." At one time the school president was Masujiro Omura, who later came to create the Meiji army, and at another time the school president was Yukichi Fukuzawa, who later became the founder of Keio University.

The Tekijuku building remains even now. The location is Kitahama 3-chome, Chuo-ku, Osaka. In those days that area consisted of merchant homes lined one after another, and the Tekijuku building was sandwiched between them. In construc-

てのただの民家だった。

　その二階が塾生のね起きの場所であった。そして教室でもあった。塾生たちは、そこでひしめくようにしてくらしていた。夏は暑かったらしい。

　先に述べた福沢諭吉は、明治以後、当時を思い出して、「ずいぶん罪のないいたずらもしたが、これ以上できないというほどに勉強もした。目が覚めれば本を読むというくらしだから、適塾にいる間、まくらというものをしたことがない。夜はつくえの横でごろねをしたのだ。」という意味のことを述べている。

　洪庵は、自分自身と弟子たちへのいましめとして、十二か条よりなる訓かいを書いた。その第一条の意味は、次のようで、まことにきびしい。

tion, it was of merchant-house style and was not what we think of as a school today. It had neither a gate nor a playground; all there was, was a two-story house. The second story was where the students slept. It was also the classroom.

The students were living there all crowded together. In summer, it appears to have been hot.

Yukichi Fukuzawa, noted above, recalled those days during the Meiji period with words to this effect. "I pulled a lot of harmless pranks, but I also studied to the point where no more could be possible. Since life consisted of reading books every waking moment, I never laid my head on a pillow. At night I dozed off by the side of my desk."

Koan wrote a set of admonitions, comprised from 12 clauses, as an exhortation to himself and his pupils.

The meaning of the first clause is as follows, and is truly severe:

医者がこの世で生活しているのは、人のためであって自分のためではない。決して有名になろうと思うな。また利益を追おうとするな。ただただ自分をすてよ。そして人を救うことだけを考えよ。

そういう洪庵に対し、幕府は、
「江戸へ来て、将軍様の侍医(奥医師)になれ。」
ということを言ってきた。目もくらむほどにめいよなことだった。奥医師というのは、日本最高の医師というだけでなく、その身分は小さな大名よりも高かったのである。つまり、洪庵の自分へのいましめに反することだった。

洪庵は断り続けた。しかし幕府は聞かず、ついに、いやいやながらそれにしたがった。

洪庵は五十三オのときに江戸へ行き、そのよく年、あっけなくなくなってしまった。

もともと病弱であったから、わかいころから体をいたわり続け、心もできるだけのどかにするよう心がけてきた。

"A doctor lives in this world for the benefit of others, not for his own benefit. Never think of becoming famous. Also, don't try to seek personal gain. Just give yourself over completely. Then think only of helping others."

The Bakufu government sent Koan a message: "Come to Edo and become the Shogun's doctor in waiting (personal physician)." This was an honor great enough to make most people giddy. To be the Shogun's personal physician was not only the top position among all doctors in Japan, it was also a status even higher than that of a minor warlord. As such, the position ran counter to Koan's self-exhortations. Koan refused repeatedly. But the Bakufu would not listen, and finally, with reluctance, he complied.

Koan, at age 53, went to Edo, and the following year he died a fleeting death. Since he had been sickly by birth, from the time he was young he continued to take special care of himself physically; he had also strived to keep his mind as peaceful as

ところが、江戸でのはなやかな生活は、洪庵の性に合わず、心ののどかさも失われてしまった。それに新しい生活が、かれに無理を強いた。それらが、かれの健康をむしばみ、江戸へ行ったよく年、火が消えるようにしてなくなったのである。

　ふり返ってみると、洪庵の一生で、最も楽しかったのは、かれが塾生たちを教育していた時代だったろう。
　洪庵は、自分の恩師たちから引きついだたいまつの火を、よりいっそう大きくした人であった。
　かれの偉大さは、自分の火を、弟子たちの一人一人に移し続けたことである。
　弟子たちのたいまつの火は、後にそれぞれの分野であかあかとかがやいた。やがてはその火の群れが、日本の近代を照らす大きな明かりになったのである。後世のわたしたちは、洪庵に感謝しなければならない。

possible. However, his flamboyant lifestyle in Edo did not agree with Koan's nature, and his peace of mind became lost. Also, his new life put a strain on him. These things gnawed away at his health, and the year after he went to Edo, he died like the sputtering of a flame.

In retrospect, the most happy time in Koan's life was probably the period when he was teaching his students. Koan was a man who took the torch he had received from his mentors and made its flame all the brighter. His greatness was his continuous passing on of his fire to each and every one of his students. The fire of his students' torches later shined brightly in their respective realms. In the end, their fires became the great light that illuminated Japan's modern era. We, the generations that followed, must be thankful to Koan.

出 典 一 覧

「人間の荘厳さ」(大阪書籍『小学国語』編集趣意書)

「21世紀に生きる君たちへ」(大阪書籍『小学国語』6年下)

「洪庵のたいまつ」(大阪書籍『小学国語』5年下)

司馬遼太郎
小説家。大阪市生まれ。『竜馬がゆく』などの歴史小説、『街道をゆく』などの歴史紀行、『この国のかたち』などのコラムと幅広く活躍。『21世紀に生きる君たちへ』『洪庵のたいまつ』は平成元年度より使われている小学校用教科書への書き下ろし。

ドナルド・キーン
アメリカの日本文学研究者。ニューヨーク生まれ。コロンビア大名誉教授。日本文学の英訳者として、近代日本文学を次々と翻訳し、日本文学が世界文学の一つとして認識される手がかりを作った。

ロバート・ミンツァー
翻訳家、コピーライター。ニュージャージ州生まれ。ハーバード大学大学院東洋言語文化学部にて文学博士号を取得

対訳　21世紀に生きる君たちへ

1999年11月10日　初版第1刷発行
2023年3月1日　初版第28刷発行
著　者　司馬遼太郎
監訳者　ドナルド・キーン
訳　者　ロバート・ミンツァー
装画装幀　安野光雅
発行者　原　雅久
発行所　朝日出版社
　　　　東京都千代田区西神田3-3-5
　　　　〒101-0065　☎03-3263-3321
印刷・製本　大日本印刷株式会社
©Midori Fukuda, Donald Keene, Robert Mintzer, 1999
Printed in Japan

乱丁、落丁はお取り替えします。無断で複写複製することは著作権の侵害になります。
定価はカバーに表示してあります。

朝日出版社の本

小さな家のローラ

ローラ・インガルス・ワイルダー 作
安野光雅 絵・監訳

緻密な描写と遊び心あふれる美しい絵と、わかりやすく親しみやすい日本語訳で、アメリカの西部開拓時代を生きた家族の、温かく力強い暮らしを忠実に描く。

文化が違っても、暮らしの本質は変わらない。いろんな場所で、いろんな人が生活している。そこには人間のドラマがある。そういう人の暮らしを描き、絵からなにかを感じ、考えてほしい。　　　　　　　　　　　　安野光雅

A5判／上製／272頁／オールカラー　定価2,750円（税込）

朝日出版社の本

赤毛のアン

ルーシイ=モード=モンゴメリ 作
岸田衿子 訳　安野光雅 絵

全世界で5,000万部突破の名作文学から新しい翻訳絵本が誕生。詩人であり童話作家であった岸田衿子氏の名訳と安野光雅氏の絵が奏でる美しいハーモニー!

人間は空想の産物。絵は想像の手助けがあって成り立つのです。
これは、アンのすぐれた想像力を大人も忘れないようにするために、読むべき一冊の本です。　安野光雅

A5判／上製／512頁／オールカラー　定価3,080円(税込)

朝日出版社の本

あしながおじさん

ジーン・ウェブスター 作

谷川俊太郎 訳　安野光雅 絵

主人公の少女ジュディ、あしながおじさん、学校の友人たち。全ての人物に作者の愛情が注がれ、変わらない温もりがこの本の中にはずっと息づいています。
少女ジュディの想像力豊かで、機転が利いてユーモアたっぷりのあしながおじさんへの数々の手紙が、谷川氏の名訳により蘇り、時代や流行、言語の違いを越えて、あたたかく読む者のこころを癒してくれます。

A5判／上製／220頁／オールカラー　定価2,420円（税込）

朝日出版社の本

メアリ・ポピンズ

トラバース 作

岸田衿子 訳　安野光雅 絵

空から舞いおりた乳母メアリ・ポピンズが、一家を不思議な世界へと導く空想物語の名作。軽やかな訳と、美しい色彩で描かれた空想あふれる絵は、心おどる世界をそっと閉じ込めて思い出させてくれます。

A5判／上製／214頁／オールカラー　定価2,420円（税込）

朝日出版社の本

ただ寄り添うだけで
岡 美穂

看護師である著者が、患者に対して、最良の対応をしていく知恵をどのように獲得していったのか？ 看護の心をわかりやすくひも解く。看護を目指す人だけでなく、看護の心を活かして生きたい人々への、ヒントとなる心のメッセージ。

B6判変型／並製／132頁　定価1,760円（税込）